The Case of the Secret Message

The Case of the Secret Message

Book created by Parker C. Hinter

Written by Michael Teitelbaum and Steve Morganstern

Illustrated by Sam Viviano

Based on characters from the Parker Brothers game

A Creative Media Applications Production

SCHOLASTIC INC.
New York Toronto London Auckland Sydney

ISBN 0-590-47907-5

22 21 20 19   2/0

Printed in the U.S.A.   40

First Scholastic printing, October 1994

Contents

Contents

The Case of the Secret Message

Introduction

Samantha Scarlet, Peter Plum, Georgie Green, Wendy White, Mortimer Mustard, and Polly Peacock are members of the Clue Club.

In this book you can match your wits with this gang of junior detectives to solve eight mysteries. Read carefully and look at each picture for clues. Can you guess who did it? Check the solution that appears upside down after the story to see if you are right!

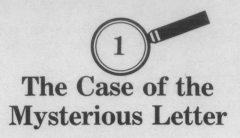

The Case of the Mysterious Letter

Wendy White sat in class tapping her foot nervously. Every few seconds she glanced up at the classroom clock.

Two fifty-five, she thought. *Only five more minutes to go!*

Wendy was not anxious just for the school day to end. She was a good student and liked her fourth-grade class. But today was a special day. Today was the day of the big Clue Jr. championship match.

Because Wendy and her five friends loved mysteries so much, they started a Clue Club. They formed the club to talk about mystery books they read, mystery TV shows and movies they like to watch, and also to play their favorite game, Clue Jr. They had planned a big match for weeks. Now the day was here, and Wendy could hardly wait.

The six-member Clue Club was divided into two teams for the competition — the Sobols, named for Donald Sobol, creator of *Encyclopedia Brown;* and the Levys, named for Elizabeth Levy, author of the *Something Queer* mysteries. Wendy was captain of the Sobols.

The bell finally rang. Wendy flew from her seat and dashed out of the classroom. In the hall, she caught up with the other members of the Clue Club.

"Are you ready to lose, Wendy?" sneered Mortimer Mustard. He was captain of the Levy team.

"Yeah, right!" said Polly Peacock. "Everyone knows that Wendy is the best player!" Polly defended her teammate, but the others could hear the jealousy in her voice.

"Wendy thinks she's so special just because her mom works at our school," snapped Mortimer.

Wendy's mother, Mrs. White, taught students who needed extra help in reading and English.

"Come on, guys," said Wendy. "That's not fair. We're all good players."

"Wendy's right," said Samantha, who was Mortimer and Peter's partner on the Levy team. "Everybody's good."

"Everybody's good," smirked Georgie, the third member of the Sobols. "It's just that we're better!"

"Actually," began Peter, "Georgie is incorrect. My careful analysis reveals that the teams are evenly matched. Although Wendy does possess remarkable deductive skills."

"Sure, egghead," said Georgie. "Whatever you said."

"Let's go, gang," said Wendy. "We don't want to be late!"

The six friends made their way through the crowd of kids rushing through the halls on their way out of the building.

The members of the Clue Club arrived at the classroom that Mr. Higgins, the school principal, had reserved for the match. Mr. Higgins himself was overseeing the competition.

"All right!" said Georgie, pulling the Clue Jr. game box from a shelf in the classroom. "Let's get the game set up."

The Clue Jr. game was set up on a long table. Three chairs were lined up on each side of the table. A Clue Jr. pad and a pencil were placed on the table in front of each chair.

Wendy, Polly, and Georgie slid into the chairs on one side of the table. Mortimer, Samantha, and Peter sat across the table.

"Go, Sobols!" cheered Georgie.

"The Levys rule!" Mortimer yelled in response.

"Actually," began Peter, misunderstanding Mortimer's cheer, "both sides must play by the rules. You see — "

The door to the classroom swung open. In walked Mr. Higgins.

Phew! thought Polly. *Good timing, Mr. Higgins. You saved us from one of Peter's long-winded lectures!*

5

Mr. Higgins looked worried.

"What's wrong, Mr. Higgins?" asked Samantha.

"I found this note in my mailbox a few minutes ago," said Mr. Higgins. He walked over to Wendy and handed her the note. "It's from your mother, Wendy. She wants you to go right home. It looks like you won't be able to play in the match."

"What?" cried Wendy. Then she read the note:

```
Wendy —
Come    home    right    after
school   today.   Some   of   my
friends  are  bringing  there
daughters  over  to  meet  you.
I'll  meet  you  their  at  3:20
sharp.   Don't   forget — its
very important.
                        Love, Mom
```

"I can't believe she would do this," said Wendy. "She knows how much this match means to me!"

Wendy -
Come home right after school today. Some of my friends are bringing there daughters over to meet you. I'll meet you their at 3:20 sharp. Don't forget-- its very important.
Love, Mom

Everyone gathered around Wendy to look at the note.

"Oh, great!" groaned Georgie. "Now we have no chance of winning!"

"Those are the breaks," sneered Mortimer, rubbing his hands with glee. *Now we'll win for sure*, he thought.

"Just a second," said Polly. She took the note from Wendy. "This was typed on a computer," she pointed out. "Wouldn't your mom have handwritten a note to you? I think this may just be a rotten trick by the Levy team to get you out of the match."

"Not necessarily, Polly," said Wendy. "My mom uses the school's computer all the time. She *could* have typed this note."

"Why don't we just call her and make sure?" asked Mr. Higgins.

"We can't, Mr. Higgins," replied Wendy. "It's 3:10. My mom would have had to leave the school at three o'clock in order to get home by 3:20 — the time in the note. She's on her way home. We can't reach her.

I guess I'd better go, so I can meet her at home."

As Wendy started to put on her coat, Polly studied the note some more, reading it over and over.

Wendy said her good-byes and left the classroom. She was very upset about having to miss the big match. She just couldn't understand why her mother would do this.

Suddenly, Polly shouted out, "Somebody go get Wendy. Quickly!"

Georgie sped from the room and caught Wendy at the end of the hall. A few seconds later they both returned.

"What's going on?" asked Wendy.

"Yes, Polly," said Mr. Higgins. "You're going to make Wendy late."

"Wendy, your mother *didn't* write this note," said Polly. "I was right. Someone on the Levy team did it to get you out of the competition! I'm sure of it!"

Can you figure out how Polly knew?

fake note. Wendy always wins, and I wanted our team to have a chance. I guess it wasn't right. I'm sorry."

"Well, Samantha," said Mr. Higgins sternly, "I'm glad you realize you made a mistake. But I'm afraid I'm going to have to disqualify you from the competition. Not only that, you apparently need extra work on spelling and grammar. I'll speak to your mother about working with you at home."

"Now it's really uphill for us Levys," Peter said. "But the game must go on."

And it did.

The Sobols' team, led by Wendy, went on to win the Clue Jr. championship. It was only fair.

Solution
The Case of the Mysterious Letter

"When I read the note carefully," Polly explained, "I found three spelling mistakes. Look at the second and third sentences. The words 'there' and 'their' are mixed up."

"That's right!" Peter said. "The writer mixed up the spelling of the adjective 'their' and the adverb 'there.' It should be spelled t-h-e-i-r in the second sentence and t-h-e-r-e in the third."

"And there's another mistake in the fourth sentence," Polly went on. "The word *its* should have an apostrophe before the s — *it's* is the contraction for the words *it is*.

"Wendy, I can't believe an English teacher like your mother would make *three* spelling mistakes like that. This note must be a fake!" concluded Polly.

"Very clever, Polly," said Mr. Higgins. Samantha's face turned bright red. "All right," she said. "You got me. I wrote the

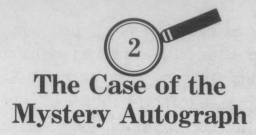

2

The Case of the Mystery Autograph

Peter Plum pounded a small gavel on the top of a wooden crate. "This meeting of the Clue Club is now in session," he said in a formal voice.

He stood behind the crate, which served as a makeshift podium, trying to look as official as he could. He gazed out at the other five members of the club, who were sitting on folding chairs in the basement of Peter's house.

"Will the secretary please read the minutes of last week's meeting?" asked Peter, looking at Samantha Scarlet.

"Thank you, Peter," said Samantha. She opened a small spiral notebook, then began to read.

"The meeting opened with Georgie

Green accusing Polly Peacock of cheating during our last Clue Jr. game. Polly then called Georgie a bully and a liar and said — I'm quoting now — 'I'm rubber, you're glue, whatever you say bounces off me and sticks to you. You're the cheater, Georgie.' End of quote."

Up at the podium, Peter rolled his eyes and shook his head. "It's good to see that our usual high level of conversation was being maintained," he said sarcastically.

Samantha continued reading the minutes. "As time ran out on the meeting last week we were starting to talk about our reports on the greatest mystery writers of all time."

"Thank you, Samantha," said Peter. "The floor is now open — "

"You'd better be careful then," interrupted Mortimer Mustard. "If the floor is open, someone might fall in. Ha-ha-ha!"

"You make that same dumb joke every week," pointed out Polly.

"Well, *I* think it's funny," said Georgie.

"Yeah, well, you would," replied Polly.

"Order! Order!" cried out Peter, pounding his gavel on the crate.

"I'll have a large pizza to go, no anchovies!" called out Mortimer. Georgie and Mortimer doubled over with laughter. The others just shook their heads impatiently.

"Oh, brother," said Samantha, turning her notebook to a fresh page and sitting down. "It's the same thing every meeting."

"Please, please," shouted Peter. "Let's begin this week's meeting. Who would like to give their report?"

"I'll start," said Wendy White, who had been sitting quietly through all the fooling around.

"Very good, Wendy," said Peter. "Thank you. The floor belongs to Wendy." Peter turned to Mortimer. "And no bad jokes, okay?"

Wendy stood up. "My report is about the great mystery writer, Sir Arthur Conan Doyle," she began. "Doyle created the world's most famous detective, Sherlock Holmes. Actually, Doyle did not start out to be a writer. He was a doctor, but during the slow times in his practice he wrote the Sherlock Holmes stories. I watch Holmes on TV. He always seems to see things that nobody else can. Little clues that help him solve the crime."

"Super, Wendy," said Peter. "Who would like to go next?"

"Me!" said Georgie, standing up. "I think Raymond Chandler is the best of the great mystery writers. He was one cool guy. Chandler's detective was Philip Marlowe, a rough, tough private eye. I like watching old movies made from Chandler's books, especially ones starring Humphrey Bogart, like *The Big Sleep*."

"Thank you, Georgie," said Peter. "I guess you *can* use your head for something other than a place to keep your hat!"

Mortimer Mustard spoke next. "I found out all about Ellery Queen. Believe it or not, Ellery Queen is not a woman or even a man. It's two men. Their real names are Frederic Dannay and Manfred Bennington Lee, and they wrote together using the pen name Ellery Queen. There was an *Ellery Queen Mystery Magazine* and a really cool TV show."

"I'll go next," said Polly, standing up. "I got to do a report on the great Agatha Christie. She created *two* famous detectives, Hercule Poirot and Miss Jane Marple."

Wendy raised her hand.

"The chair recognizes Wendy White," said Peter.

"What about the table?" whispered Mortimer. Both he and Georgie started to giggle.

Wendy ignored them and opened up her backpack. "I was hoping that someone would do a report on Agatha Christie," she began.

Polly looked on with great interest as Wendy pulled a framed piece of paper out of her backpack.

"My uncle Geoffrey was actually a close, personal friend of Agatha Christie," explained Wendy.

"No way," said Georgie.

"Shut up, Georgie," snapped Polly. "Let her talk."

"Anyway," Wendy continued, "it turns out that Ms. Christie gave my uncle an autograph. It's rare and very valuable. She didn't give out many autographs. My uncle was very honored. In fact, it's a White family heirloom. But since you're such a big fan, Polly, and you're my pal, I'd be willing to swap it for that new sweater you got for your birthday last week."

"Wow!" exclaimed Polly. "Agatha Christie's autograph. Let's see."

Wendy handed the framed paper to Polly. The others gathered around, staring wide-eyed in amazement. The beautiful gold antique frame had a delicate pattern of vines and flowers running around its four sides. What was *in* the frame was even more impressive.

Within the gold frame sat a ragged piece of writing paper which had turned yellow with age. In the center of the paper, written in a fine script were the following words:

To my dear friend,
Geoffrey
White
with warmest
regards,
Agatha Christie
November 31, 1956

To my dear friend, Geoffrey White,
with warmest regards

At the bottom, it was signed:

Agatha Christie, November 31, 1956

"It's wonderful," said Samantha. "She had such lovely handwriting."

"It looks real to me," added Georgie. "The paper sure looks like it's almost forty years old, and the frame is even older."

"Of course it's real," said Wendy. "What do you think, Polly? Are you interested in swapping?"

"I'd sure love to have it, Wendy," replied Polly. "Although I do like my new sweater, and it was a birthday present from my favorite aunt. Still, it's tempting."

"Just a minute, Polly," said Mortimer, who was holding the autograph and studying it carefully. "I don't think you should do this."

"Why not?" asked Polly, who had just

about decided to go ahead and make the trade.

"Because this autograph is not real," replied Mortimer. "It's a fraud!"

Do you know why Mortimer thinks the autograph is phony?

Solution
The Case of the Mystery Autograph

The members of the Clue Club were shocked.

"What do you mean it's a fraud?" said Wendy, who acted very offended by Mortimer's charge. "This has been in my family for decades."

"This autograph is dated November 31, 1956," began Mortimer. "Remember the old rhyme 'Thirty days hath September, April, June, and November?' There is no November 31. I think Wendy wrote this herself."

Wendy turned bright red with embarrassment. "Drat!" she exclaimed. "How could I make such a stupid mistake? If I had picked any other date, my forgery would have worked. I'm sorry, Polly. I knew you liked Agatha Christie. I thought you'd never know the autograph wasn't genuine."

"How did you make it look so real?" Polly asked.

"The last time I was looking around in my family's musty old attic I found this antique frame. I also found a few sheets of old writing paper. I decided to fake the autograph, put it in the frame, and see if I could fool you guys. I'm really sorry. That's the last time I'll ever try anything like this. I promise."

"I don't know if I believe you," said Polly. "Can I get that in writing?"

The Case of the Disappearing Cat

It was a clear, sunny Sunday morning. All of the members of the Clue Club were very busy. The next day, the annual pet talent show was going to be held in the school auditorium. Each of the club members had a pet that could do some kind of unusual trick.

Peter Plum had taught his dog, Bizzy, to walk all the way across a room on his hind legs.

Wendy White's pet parrot, Petunia, could sing all the words to "Happy Birthday to You."

Mortimer Mustard's goldfish, Jaws, swam through a series of hoops in his fish tank whenever Mortimer fed him.

Polly Peacock had a turtle, Speedo, who was able to climb to the top of a papier-mâché mountain Polly had made and come sliding down a chute on the other side.

Georgie Green's monkey, Bingo, was learning to juggle.

And Samantha Scarlet's cat, Mittens, could walk across a long balance beam.

All morning long, each member of the club was hard at work, perfecting the pet trick that would win the talent contest.

Samantha had a ten-foot-long, two-inch-wide balance beam set up in her backyard. She sat next to Mittens at one end of the beam. The cat was bright orange, except for his four white paws.

"Good kitty," she said, scratching Mittens gently between his eyes. He purred loudly. "Let's try it again."

Samantha went to the opposite end of the beam. "Come on, Mittens," she called. "Hop on and do your stuff!"

Mittens let out a soft purr, then stepped up onto the narrow beam. Walking briskly, he placed one paw in front of the other. It only took him a few moments to reach the other end. He hopped off the beam and rubbed up against Samantha.

"You are the best little kitty in the whole world," cooed Samantha. "Yes, you are. And we're going to win that talent contest tomorrow."

"Samantha!" came a voice from the house. It was her mom. "It's twelve o'clock. Time for lunch. Come in now. You can practice again with Mittens after lunch."

"I'll be right in, Mom," Samantha called back. "Now you wait right here, Mittens. I'll be out in a little while."

Mittens purred and meowed. Then he strolled over to his favorite spot, under a big oak tree, and curled up into a fluffy orange ball.

Samantha went into the house.

A short while later, after gulping down a peanut butter sandwich and a glass of milk, Samantha ran out into the backyard. Mittens was nowhere in sight.

"Mittens!" she called. "Are you hiding, you silly cat?"

Samantha searched the whole backyard but there was no trace of Mittens. "Where can he be?" she cried. "He'd never run away. And he didn't just disappear."

Samantha noticed that her next-door neighbor, Mrs. Lavender, was working in her garden.

"Excuse me, Mrs. Lavender," said Samantha, leaning over the wooden fence that separated their backyards.

"Why, what is it, Samantha, dear?" asked Mrs. Lavender. "You look terribly upset."

"Have you seen Mittens? I left him in our yard at lunchtime."

"No," said Mrs. Lavender, "I haven't seen Mittens today." She thought for a second.

"But I did see a boy in your yard earlier," she said.

"A boy?" asked Samantha. "What did he look like?"

"Well, I only got a quick glance at his back as he was leaving," explained Mrs. Lavender. "But I think he had light-brown hair. Yes, and he was wearing a green jacket and green pants."

"Georgie Green!" exclaimed Samantha, getting very angry. "I should have known. He's always been jealous of Mittens' great talent. I'll bet he kidnapped my little kitty. He just wants his stupid monkey to win the talent show. Thanks, Mrs. Lavender."

Samantha dashed into the house and quickly called Peter, Wendy, Mortimer, and Polly. She asked them all to meet her at Georgie's house. Together they would force Georgie to admit his crime.

They all rode their bikes to Georgie's house and met outside. Samantha stormed up to the front door and rang the bell.

"Oh, hi, guys," said Georgie. "What's up?"

"You," said Samantha angrily. "Up to no good!"

"What are you talking about?" asked Georgie.

"A little while ago," began Samantha, "around noon, you came to my house and took Mittens!"

"That's not true," said Georgie. "I was right here all morning. And I can prove it!"

Georgie invited the members of the Clue Club into his house. They gathered around the television set in the living room.

"It just so happens, Miss Samantha Smarty-pants, that today at noon, I was working with Bingo, in my yard," said Georgie. "I thought it would be helpful to videotape him, so I set up my camera on a tripod and shot our practice session. Here, look."

Georgie slipped a videocassette into the VCR and hit PLAY. Up on the big screen came the images of Georgie and Bingo. Bingo was trying to juggle three balls, but he kept dropping one. Georgie chased after the dropped balls and tossed them back to the monkey.

"You see the time and date listed right there on the tape," said Georgie, pointing to the lower right-hand corner of the screen. "It says 'Sunday, October 5, 12:03 P.M.' That's where I was when your stupid cat was taken."

"But you can hardly see Bingo," pointed out Mortimer. "The trees are casting such long shadows that he's completely in the shade!"

"I realized that, after a few minutes," explained Georgie. "So we moved inside to continue practicing where I could get a better video image. Look, I'll fast forward the tape a bit."

Georgie sped through the tape. The scene changed from the backyard to the Green family's basement. The lighting was better indoors, and the image of Bingo juggling was clear.

"Look at the time and date now," said Georgie. The bottom right-hand corner now said SUNDAY, OCTOBER 5, 12:07 P.M.

"And look at the clock on the basement wall," continued Georgie. The clock clearly said 12:07 P.M., too.

"And there you have my airtight alibi," smirked Georgie. "On the screen, in living color. So you see, I was right here around noon. I couldn't possibly be the pet-napper."

SUNDAY OCTOBER 5 12:07 P.M.

"It's possible to change the time on the video camera and on the clock," said Polly, looking for a flaw in Georgie's argument.

"Oh, yeah?" snapped Georgie. "Well, let's see you prove it!"

During all this, Peter Plum had been sitting quietly. He tapped his temple with his finger. He scrunched his face up, deep in thought. He now spoke up for the first time.

"I think I can prove that you changed the time on the video and the clock," said Peter. "Rewind the tape, Georgie. Let's look at it again from the beginning."

Can you figure out why Peter thinks Georgie changed the time on the video?

was coming along with her trick, and there was the cat, walking back and forth on the beam like a champion. I couldn't resist taking him. I was only going to keep him under wraps until the show was over. It would have been less competition for Bingo."

"Georgie Green, that was a mean trick," Samantha said. "But you should have known you couldn't get away with that phony alibi. After all, we're the Clue Club."

"You're right," Georgie said. "You guys are too smart."

Georgie brought Mittens out of the bedroom and handed him over to Samantha.

"Thanks, Peter," said Samantha, as she cuddled the cat in her arms. "You really shed some light on this crime!"

Solution
The Case of the Disappearing Cat

Georgie rewound the tape and everyone watched it again.

"There, stop the tape," said Peter. Georgie paused the tape. It stopped on a freeze-frame of Bingo under the shadows cast by the trees.

"Look," continued Peter. "At the time this tape was shot, the trees were casting long shadows, making it hard to see Bingo. But at noon, the time Georgie claimed it was shot, the sun is always directly overhead, so the trees would cast hardly any shadows at all.

"These scenes were obviously not shot at noon, and Georgie obviously changed the time on the video camera and on the clock."

"So your alibi is a lie!" exclaimed Samantha.

"All right," said Georgie, throwing up his hands in defeat. "I 'borrowed' Mittens. I had just gone over to see how Samantha

The Case of the Missing Cake

Each week the Clue Club met in a different member's home. This week's meeting was being held in the game room of the Mustard Mansion. As usual, the six members of the club had divided into two teams for a few rousing games of Clue Jr. Georgie Green's team had just won their third game in a row.

"Well, I've had enough losing for one night," said Wendy White.

"But you're the best player, Wendy," said her teammate Samantha Scarlet. "What happened?"

"I don't know, Samantha," replied Wendy. "I guess anyone can have an off night."

"I just think that I'm a better detective than you are," taunted Polly Peacock,

Georgie's teammate on the winning team.

"Let's not get into this argument again," said Mortimer Mustard, who was also on the losing team.

"Every week, whoever wins goes on bragging about being the best detective," continued Mortimer. "Frankly, the whole thing bores me. Now, who's up for a snack?"

At the mention of a snack, all discussion about who was the best detective stopped.

"Now that's the best idea anyone's had all evening," commented Peter Plum. "Unless, of course, you're planning on serving cookies or cake or ice cream."

"Here we go again," sneered Polly.

"Well, it's just that I prefer healthy snacks like fruit or whole wheat crackers," explained Peter.

"Don't worry, Peter," said Mortimer. "There'll be something for everyone."

"Hey!" said Polly. "That reminds me. Tomorrow is Ms. Redding's birthday." Ms. Redding was their fourth-grade teacher. "My sister was in her class last year. She told me that on her birthday, Ms. Redding brought in a special surprise treat for the whole class. Maybe she'll do it again this year."

"Great!" said Georgie. "I wonder what the surprise will be."

The next morning, the six Clue Club members were in their seats even before Ms. Redding arrived.

"I hope she brings éclairs," said Georgie. "I just love éclairs."

"I hope it's those fancy bakery cookies," said Samantha. "The kind with the jelly in the middle and the sprinkles on top."

"Nah!" said Polly. "I want a huge tub of butter pecan ice cream."

"Strawberry shortcake," murmured Wendy. "With lots of whipped cream."

"Stop it, you guys," said Mortimer. "I'm never going to make it to lunch!"

"Personally," began Peter, "some stone-ground crackers topped with fresh mango slices would be just delightful."

Before anyone could comment on Peter's

taste in treats, Ms. Redding walked into the classroom.

"Good morning, class," she said cheerfully. "Before we begin today's lessons, I have a surprise for you."

The members of the Clue Club gave the thumbs-up sign to each other.

"Today is my birthday," explained Ms. Redding.

"Happy birthday, Ms. Redding," the whole class said together.

"Thank you very much," replied Ms. Redding. "Every year, I like to bring the class a special surprise treat to celebrate my special day." She held up a big bakery box.

Oohs and *ahhs* filled the classroom.

"I'm afraid, however," Ms. Redding continued, "that we'll have to wait until this afternoon — after you've eaten a good lunch. So, I'll just put this box here on the corner of my desk.

"Now, if you'll open your math books to page sixty-eight, we'll begin today's lesson."

Grunts and groans replaced the *oohs* and *ahhs* as the students opened their books, and the morning's lessons began.

After what seemed like weeks to everyone who was busy thinking about the special treat, the bell for lunch period finally rang.

The students burst from the classroom. Some went to the school cafeteria to buy their lunches, others took the sandwiches they had brought from home and ate them out in the playground.

When the class returned, Ms. Redding turned to the bakery box on her desk. "It's treat time!" she said, flipping open the lid.

She looked into the box and gasped. "Oh, no!" she cried. "The cake. It's gone!"

The students in the class turned to each other with accusing looks.

"I can't believe this!" exclaimed Ms. Redding. "Someone must have sneaked into the empty classroom during lunch period and eaten the entire cake! Would anyone like to confess?"

No one answered.

"Very well, then," she said. "I'm going to have to ask each of you where you were during lunch period. Maybe we'll get to the truth that way."

One by one the students offered their alibis.

"I was playing basketball in the playground with Mortimer," said Georgie.

"That's true, Ms. Redding," said Mortimer. "We were together for the entire lunch period."

"I was in the cafeteria, reading," said Wendy.

"I ate my lunch quickly, then spent the rest of the period in the computer room, Ms. Redding," said Peter.

"I was in the school library, working on my history assignment," said Polly. "Besides, I'm allergic to chocolate, anyway. If I had eaten the cake, I'd be covered with red blotches by now."

"I was in the playground playing jump rope with my friends from Ms. Mauve's class," said Samantha.

Ms. Redding listened to every student

in her class. No one admitted to eating the cake.

"Well," said Ms. Redding. "It seems our treat got up and walked out of the room all by itself!"

Wendy raised her hand. "No, Ms. Redding," she said. "I know who ate the cake!"

How did Wendy know?

think I ate too much. My stomach doesn't feel so good."

"Who's the best detective now, Polly?" Wendy taunted. "The teacher brings in a special treat for the whole class and you eat it all yourself! That really takes the cake!"

Solution
The Case of the Missing Cake

"Are you confessing, Wendy?" asked Ms. Redding.

"No, Ms. Redding," replied Wendy. "Polly Peacock ate the snack. I can prove it."

"That's ridiculous," said Polly.

"No, Polly, it's true," said Wendy. "Ms. Redding never said that the cake was *chocolate*. And she never showed it to us. Only the person who ate it could know that."

"That's right, Wendy," said Ms. Redding. "An excellent bit of detective work. Polly, what have you got to say for yourself?"

Polly's face turned bright red.

"She's right," admitted Polly. "I came back in after everyone went to lunch just to see what was in the box. I only meant to look, but before I knew it, I'd eaten the whole cake! I never went to the library. I'm not really allergic to chocolate, but I

The Case of
Movie Madness

The weekly meeting of the Clue Club was in session. It was Friday night. Everyone was excited because the next day they were going to the opening of a brand-new mystery movie.

"Quick!" shouted Polly Peacock. "Open the paper to the movie section!"

Georgie Green spread the local newspaper wide open on the table. "Let's see," began Georgie, flipping through the paper. "Here they are. The movie listings."

Polly sat down next to Georgie and began to read the movie titles. "*Attack of the French Fries from Jupiter, Really Stupid Proposal, That Wacky Bob — The Movie, Part 2!* Ah, here it is. *The Mystery of the Black Veil.*"

"My parents saw it," said Mortimer Mustard. "They said it's great."

"I love mystery movies," said Wendy White.

"The part I enjoy most about mystery movies," added Peter Plum, "is trying to figure out the ending."

"That's when you know how good a detective you really are," said Samantha Scarlet.

Polly looked at the movie ad in the paper. "The first show is at twelve noon tomorrow," she announced. "Let's meet at the theater at eleven-thirty so we have enough time to buy our tickets and get good seats."

"Yeah!" exclaimed Georgie. "I want to sit in the front row!"

"That sounds cool to me," added Mortimer.

"Well, I don't know," Peter said nervously. "Sitting that close can actually do long-term damage to your vision. I just finished reading a study in the *American*

Journal of Medicine. It's really quite fascinating. They say that — "

"MEETING   ADJOURNED!!!"   the other five club members all shouted together. They knew that Peter was about to launch into one of his endless lectures.

"Very funny," said Peter. "I get your point. I was just going to explain — "

"Peter!" exclaimed Polly.

"All right, all right," replied Peter. "Meeting adjourned."

"Okay, guys," said Georgie. "We'll meet at eleven-thirty at the theater. See you tomorrow."

The meeting ended, and the club members headed for home.

The next morning at 11:30, the six friends met outside the Multi-Plex Cinema and got on the long line of kids who arrived early to buy tickets.

"I'm glad we got here early," said Polly. "It looks like it's going to be a full house."

After waiting on line for a few minutes, Wendy reached the ticket seller. She opened her purse and counted out her money. "Oh, no," she said in a panicky voice. "I forgot to bring all my money. I only have two dollars and seventy-five cents. But the children's admission price is three dollars!"

"Don't worry, Wendy," said Samantha, who was right behind her on line. "I have an extra quarter. Here."

Samantha reached into her pocket, pulled out a quarter, and handed it to Wendy. Wendy bought her ticket and went inside. Each of the other club members did the same, and the friends had soon regrouped in the theater's lobby.

They gave their tickets to the ticket taker and proceeded into the theater.

"I want to sit in the front row," said Georgie.

"I refuse," said Peter. "I'm going to the back of the theater where I won't ruin my eyes."

"I'm going with Georgie," said Mortimer.

"I'll sit with Peter," said Wendy.

"Hold on, guys," said Samantha. "We're

47

a club. We should stick together. Let's just all sit in the middle."

After a bit more arguing, they finally agreed with Samantha. The six club members were soon settled into their seats, waiting for the movie to begin.

Suddenly the usher, a teenaged boy, came storming into the theater. "All right. Everybody up and out into the lobby!"

A confused buzzing filled the theater.

"Some kid was seen sneaking into the theater through the side door," the usher continued. "So I need to get all of you out into the lobby so I can check your ticket stubs."

The crowd of kids filed from their seats out into the lobby.

As Peter Plum passed the usher, he stopped. "If someone saw the kid sneak in," Peter asked, "then why don't you know who it is?"

"Listen, wise guy," snapped the usher. "What are you, some kind of detective or something?"

"Well, actually," began Peter, "I pride myself on — "

"I don't care, kid!" barked the usher. "But if you have to know, the back door opens outside into the bright daylight, so it was impossible to get a good look at who was sneaking in. The kid just slipped into the crowd. Now step out into the lobby with everyone else!"

The six club members, along with all the other kids who had come to see the movie, were soon lined up in the lobby. One by one the usher checked their ticket stubs.

"Hey!" Georgie said to Peter. "Isn't that Bobby Blue, that tough kid who's always getting into trouble?" Georgie pointed at a tall kid wearing a black leather jacket who was a few feet ahead of them on line.

"Yeah!" whispered Peter. "I'll bet he's the one who snuck in."

But when the usher got to Bobby Blue, he glanced at Bobby's ticket stub and waved him through. Peter peeked over Bobby's shoulder at his stub. Bobby just smiled and slipped it into his pocket.

When the usher got to Wendy, she fumbled around in her pockets. She had forgotten where she put her ticket stub. "I can't believe it," cried Wendy. "I'm always forgetting everything. Now I can't find the stub."

"All right," the usher said to Wendy. "You wait on the side."

When he had finished checking all the kids, it turned out that Wendy was the only one without a stub. "Let's go," said the usher. "I'm taking you to the manager."

"Wait a minute!" shouted Peter. "You've got the wrong person. And I can prove it!"

How did Peter know?

get into trouble, when she didn't do any-thing wrong."

"You know what, kid?" said the usher. "As much as I hate to admit it, you're right!"

The usher took Bobby Blue to the man-ager's office. Wendy and the rest of the kids filed back into the theater.

"Thanks, Peter," said Wendy once they were seated. "You really solved that mys-tery. I only hope that the detective in *The Mystery of the Black Veil* is as smart as you are!"

Solution
The Case of Movie Madness

"What are you talking about, smart guy?" asked the usher.

"I saw the ticket stub that Bobby Blue was holding," explained Peter. "Check it again."

The usher called Bobby over and checked his stub again.

"If you look at it closely, you'll see that it is a seven-dollar-and-fifty-cent adult-price ticket," said Peter. "If Bobby had bought a ticket he would have only had to pay the children's admission price of three dollars, like the rest of us.

"I believe that Bobby is the one who snuck in. He then picked up a stub from the theater floor without even looking to see if it was a children's ticket. He got this adult ticket stub just by chance.

"I wasn't going to say anything at first because Bobby is so much bigger than me," said Peter. "I was afraid. But I couldn't just stand by and watch my friend Wendy

53

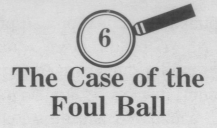

The Case of the
Foul Ball

It was a hot, humid Saturday. The whole Clue Club gang was at Georgie Green's house.

"Nice going, Georgie," kidded Mortimer Mustard. "You picked the hottest day in history to invite us over."

"Stop being such a baby, Mortimer," Georgie shot back. "Come on, everyone. Let's play some baseball."

Georgie held his bat and ball. He was ready for an afternoon of sports.

"No thank you, Georgie," said Peter Plum. "I'd prefer to sit under a shady tree and read. I've just started this fascinating book about the history of stamp collecting. Why, do you know — "

"I'm sure we don't, Peter," interrupted Georgie.

"I think Peter's right, though," said Samantha Scarlet. "It's too hot for me. I'm all for relaxing in the shade."

"How about watching a mystery movie?" asked Polly Peacock.

"Georgie's got some great movies on tape," said Wendy White. "How about it, Georgie?"

"You guys can watch a movie if you want," said Georgie. "But I'm playing baseball. If no one wants to play with me, I'll just play with Bingo."

Georgie went to the garage and brought Bingo out into the backyard. Georgie tossed him the ball, and the monkey pitched it back. Georgie smacked the ball with his bat and Bingo happily chased it and brought it back.

Meanwhile, Peter found a shady spot under a large maple tree and settled down comfortably to read.

Wendy, Samantha, Polly, and Mortimer

were inside the house watching *And Then There Were None* on Georgie's big-screen TV.

"This is my favorite old movie," said Polly. "It's from a story by Agatha Christie."

All the Clue Club members were enjoying themselves when Bingo became bored with playing baseball with Georgie. He decided it would be more fun to annoy Peter.

Instead of bringing the ball back to Georgie, Bingo climbed the maple tree and dropped the ball right on Peter's head.

"Hey!" shouted Peter. "What is wrong with Bingo?" Peter was naturally upset to be hit on the head with a ball.

"I guess he just likes you, Peter," said Georgie, trying to hide the fact that he was giggling.

"I fail to see humor in annoying others," stated Peter.

"That's because you do it so often yourself," replied Georgie.

Peter ignored this rude remark and went back to reading his book.

But Bingo was far from finished. During the rest of the day he continued to torment Peter.

He snatched the book right from Peter's hands.

"Hey!" yelled Peter. "Give that back!"

Bingo dashed off with the book, leading Peter on a chase around and around the house. When Peter was completely out of breath, Bingo finally gave him back his book.

When Peter got comfortable under the tree again, Bingo poked him with the baseball bat.

Peter jumped up and started yelling at Georgie. "This monkey of yours is driving me crazy!" he complained.

"That's just what my mother has been saying for weeks," explained Georgie. "Bingo broke her favorite vase last week. My mom said that if he caused any more damage he would have to go. Bingo is not allowed in the house anymore. He has to sleep in the garage."

"Well, I wish he'd stay in the garage *all* the time," said Peter. "I'm going into the house. At least Bingo won't bother me there!"

A short while later Georgie came into the house. He put the bat down and found the others watching the end of the movie. All except for Peter. He was curled up on the couch reading his book.

"Listen, Peter," said Georgie. "I'm sorry about Bingo. Let me make it up to you. I know you'd like to be better at sports. Let me help you with your hitting."

Peter was proud of being a "brain," but he had always secretly wanted to be a good ballplayer, too. Georgie knew this.

"All right," agreed Peter. "That's very nice of you. Just let me finish this page and I'll be right out."

"Great!" said Georgie. "We'll meet you outside. You bring the bat."

Georgie headed for the garage to get

baseball gloves, while everyone else went around to the backyard.

Suddenly they heard a crash from the front of the house. They all raced around from the backyard.

As Polly ran, she tripped over a small bush that was at the side of the house.

"Are you all right?" asked Wendy.

"I'm fine," replied Polly. "I wasn't watching where I was going. Come on, let's see what happened!"

When they reached the front of the house, they discovered that a living room window had been smashed to pieces. Peter stood in the front yard holding the bat and shaking his head.

"That mischievous monkey!" Peter exclaimed. "He threw the ball right through the living room window."

The club members went into the house. The ball Bingo had been playing with was now in the middle of the living room floor.

"This looks really bad for Bingo," said

Georgie. "When my mom sees this, he's going to be in big trouble."

The gang went back outside. Wendy carefully stepped up to the broken window to investigate. Pieces of broken glass crunched under her feet.

"Be careful, guys," said Wendy. "There's broken glass all over the front lawn."

"Broken glass?" asked Samantha. She carefully tiptoed up to the window and examined the area. "Did anybody let Bingo into the house?"

They all shook their heads.

Georgie was very upset. He spoke to Bingo in a stern voice. "That was really dumb, Bingo," he said. "Mom's going to make me get rid of you when she sees what you did."

"I don't think you have to worry about that," said Samantha, who had completed her investigation.

"What do you mean?" asked Georgie.

"Bingo didn't do this," stated Samantha.

"He didn't?" asked a surprised Georgie.
"No," replied Samantha. "But I know who did!"

Who did it? And how did Samantha know?

Solution
The Case of the Foul Ball

"Since no one let Bingo into the house, he could have only thrown the ball from the outside," began Samantha. "From the location of the ball in the living room, it appears that that's what happened.

"However, if the ball was thrown from the outside, the broken glass would be *inside* the house. This shattered glass is outside, on the front lawn. That means the window was broken from the inside. There was only one person inside when that happened."

Peter Plum sighed. "All right," he said. "You got me. *I* broke the window, not Bingo. After everyone went out, I picked up the bat that Georgie had left in the living room. I was just taking a couple of practice swings — but I must have swung too hard. The bat flew out of my hands and smashed right through the window. I ran outside and picked up the bat. That's when I noticed Bingo's ball lying on the lawn.

I was annoyed at him for bothering me all day, so I put his ball in the living room to make it look as if he had thrown the ball.

"I tried to frame him but, Samantha, you were just too good a detective for me to get away with it."

Peter agreed to pay for the window out of his allowance.

"Anyone for a game of baseball?" asked Georgie. "Peter can lead off since he's so good with the bat."

"Very funny, Georgie," said Peter.

"Very funny."

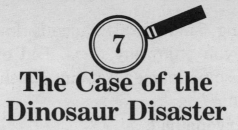

The Case of the
Dinosaur Disaster

Ms. Redding stood in front of her fourth-grade class, which included all the Clue Club members.

"Good morning, class," said Ms. Redding. "As you all know, today we're going on a field trip. To tie in with our unit on dinosaurs, we will be going to the Natural History Museum to look at their fabulous dinosaur exhibit. They have some marvelous models that will help you get an idea of what the dinosaurs were like. We will be spending the entire morning at the museum."

The whole class cheered.

"A whole morning out of school," Georgie Green whispered to Mortimer Mustard. "Yes!"

"All right, class, settle down," said Ms.

Redding, smiling. "It's nice to know how much you enjoy my class. Did everyone bring some money to buy lunch at the museum?"

Everyone had.

"Good," said Ms. Redding. "Then we're all set. Let's form a line and go out to the bus."

The class lined up and walked, single file, from the classroom. When they got outside, the members of the Clue Club, along with their classmates, piled onto the school bus.

"Listen up, class," called out Ms. Redding when all of her students had found seats. "There are a few things you'll need to know when we get to the museum. I want you to all stay together in a group and, most importantly, do not touch anything. We are there to look, not to touch."

The bus driver closed the doors, and the bus headed off for the museum.

"This is going to be great!" exclaimed Samantha Scarlet, who was sitting next to Polly Peacock.

"My favorite dinosaur is the tricera-tops," said Polly. "I think those horns on its head are cool."

Georgie Green and Wendy White were in the seats behind Polly and Samantha.

"No way," said Georgie. "T-rex is the coolest. He had teeth that were ten inches long and could rip the flesh right off your body."

"Yuk," whined Wendy. "That's disgust-ing. I like the brontosaurus best. He had a long beautiful neck and tail. And besides, he was a vegetarian."

Peter Plum and Mortimer Mustard sat behind Georgie and Wendy.

"Actually," began Peter, "the term *brontosaurus* is no longer used. The di-nosaur that you are referring to is more properly known as *apatosaurus*."

"A-PAT-o-saurus?" repeated Mortimer. "How about a pat on your back?" Mortimer slapped Peter's back with his palm. "Got you last!" said Mortimer.

"Why do you insist on playing this stupid 'got you last' game, Mortimer?" whined

Peter. "I really don't want to play. I — oh, my, look!" Peter pointed out the window. "A pterodactyl!"

"Where?" shouted Mortimer, craning his neck to see out the window.

"Got you last!" said Peter, smiling.

Mortimer and Peter played "got you last" during the entire bus ride.

Finally the bus arrived at the museum. The doors opened and the class filed out, lining up on the museum's front steps. Then they went into the museum where they were met by Mr. Black, the museum tour guide.

"Welcome, children," began Mr. Black. "I'll be leading you on a tour of our dinosaur exhibit. We'll meet the largest and the smallest dinosaurs, the gentle plant-eaters, and the ferocious meat-eaters. I hope you'll learn a lot, and that you'll have fun doing it. Now, let's begin."

The class visited the exhibits for many different types of dinosaurs.

"This is the stegosaurus," explained Mr. Black. He stood in front of a scale model of a stegosaurus skeleton. "It had bony plates running along its back and a spiked tail. They were used as protection from the huge meat-eaters of the time."

"Like T-rex?" asked Georgie.

"Actually, " replied Mr. Black, "T-rex lived in a different time period than stegosaurus. The meat-eating ceratosaurus would probably have been the dinosaur that hunted stegosaurus.

"Now if you'll all follow me, we'll move on to the next dinosaur."

As the group moved from exhibit to exhibit, Mortimer and Peter continued their "got you last" game. Mortimer opened the zipper on Peter's backpack, and all his books fell out onto the floor.

"Got you last!" whispered Mortimer, as Peter knelt down to pick up his books.

At the velociraptor exhibit, Peter shoved Mortimer from behind. As Mortimer stumbled forward, he bumped into the model of the dinosaur.

"Mortimer!" said Ms. Redding, staring angrily at him. "You know you're not supposed to touch the exhibits. Now please behave."

"Got you last!" said Peter, after Mortimer apologized.

"The velociraptor," Mr. Black said, "was a deadly hunter who hunted in packs. It was a swift and powerful killer, and one of the most intelligent of the dinosaurs of the Cretaceous Period."

The tour ended at the tyrannosaurus rex exhibit. In the center of the exhibit stood an eight-foot-tall scale model of a T-rex skeleton. It was upright, in a fighting position; its huge jaws opened menacingly; its tiny arms held up in the air.

"Now this is what *I* came to see," said Georgie. "He is the coolest."

"Tyrannosaurus rex," said Mr. Black. "Its name says it all. It means 'king of the thunder lizards.' It was the most feared of all the dinosaurs. It was forty feet long and eighteen feet tall when it stood on its hind legs, like our model here."

Mr. Black ended his tour. "You've been

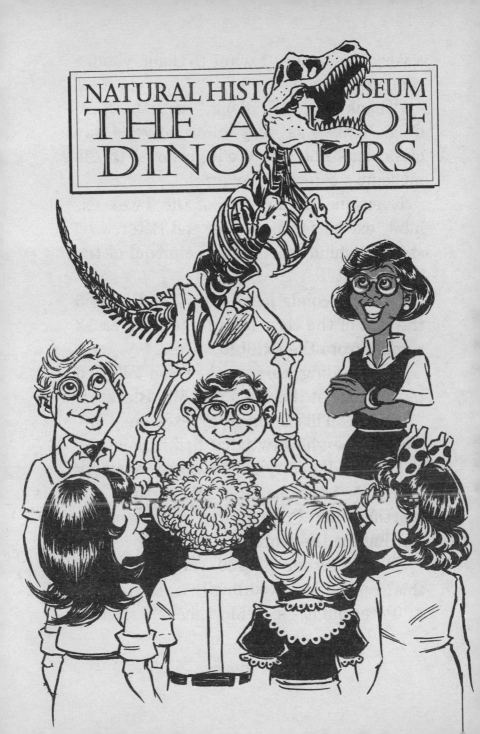

a very nice group. I want to thank you for coming."

"Thank you, Mr. Black," said Ms. Redding. "This was very informative. Okay class, let's line up. We'll go down to the museum's cafeteria for lunch."

Everyone walked out of the T-rex exhibit, except for Mortimer and Peter, who stayed behind staring at the model of the huge beast.

A few seconds later, Ms. Redding and the rest of the class heard a terrible crash coming from the exhibit room.

Ms. Redding ran into the room followed by the rest of the class and Mr. Black.

"Oh, no! This is terrible!" exclaimed Mr. Black, when he saw what had happened.

The model T-rex had come crashing down. Its bones sat in a pile on the floor. Mortimer and Peter glared at each other, waiting for the worst.

"Would either of you care to explain this?" asked Ms. Redding in a stern voice.

"Peter did it," said Mortimer. "I tried to

stop him, but he wanted to take a sample bone from the model for Georgie, because Georgie liked the T-rex so much. He grabbed the model by the arm and pulled really hard. The whole thing came crashing to the ground."

"Young man, you are coming with me," Mr. Black said to Peter. "We are going to call your parents."

"Hey, wait a minute — " Peter began.

"I don't want to hear any excuses," said Mr. Black. "It's going to take weeks to rebuild the model. You just deprived many other museum visitors of the pleasure of seeing one of our most popular exhibits."

"Hold everything," said Georgie Green, stepping forward. "Mortimer is lying!"

How did Georgie know that Mortimer was lying?

Solution
The Case of the Dinosaur Disaster

"I am not lying," said Mortimer.

"Well then, explain this," Georgie began. "You said that Peter grabbed the T-rex by the arm. But the model is in a standing position. The arms must be almost six feet high. It would be impossible for Peter to have reached that high. Therefore you must be lying."

"Thank you, Georgie," said Peter. "I was trying to tell you that Mortimer knocked the entire model over. He tried to put the blame on me to get me in trouble."

As Mr. Black led Mortimer away to the museum office, Peter added, "Oh, by the way, Mortimer. GOT YOU LAST!"

74

The Case of the
Secret Message

All the members of the Clue Club were at Samantha Scarlet's house. They had finished their meeting and wanted to play in the park across town.

"Mom, can you drive us to the park?" asked Samantha. "We're bored. We want to play soccer."

"Yeah," said Mortimer Mustard. "Boys against girls!"

"You got it!" shouted back Polly Peacock.

"I can drop you all at the park," said Mrs. Scarlet, "but I have a very important stop on the way. I'll tell you about it in the car."

Samantha, Polly, Mortimer, Peter, Wendy, and Georgie piled into Mrs. Scarlet's station wagon, and off they drove.

"Where are we stopping, Mom?" asked Samantha.

"Do you remember Mrs. Turquoise?" began Mrs. Scarlet.

"The piano teacher?" asked Samantha. "She's been in this town forever. Didn't you take lessons from her when you were a kid?"

"That's right," replied Mrs. Scarlet.

"Are we going to see her, Mrs. Scarlet?" asked Peter.

"Well, actually, Peter," began Mrs. Scarlet, "Mrs. Turquoise recently passed away. She was quite old. I'm the lawyer in charge of settling her estate. Her family was always very wealthy, so there's a lot of money involved."

"Didn't she live in that big spooky house on the edge of town?" asked Georgie.

"That's where we're stopping," explained Mrs. Scarlet. "I promised Mrs. Turquoise that I would feed her parrot, Gabe. Toward the end of her life, Gabe was Mrs. Turquoise's only companion."

Mrs. Scarlet's face grew serious.

"What's the matter, Mom?" asked Samantha. "You look worried about something."

"I *am* concerned," said Mrs. Scarlet, taking a deep breath. "You see, nobody has been able to find Mrs. Turquoise's will. Her will explains what she wanted to do with all her money. She never really trusted lawyers and banks, and so she hid her will somewhere in her house.

"I've searched the house from top to bottom, but I've had no luck finding the will. And just this week Mrs. Turquoise's nephew, Uriah, started demanding that the court award him all of her money. Mrs. Turquoise mentioned to me several times that she intended to leave her money to charity. I'm afraid that without a will to prove that, Uriah has a very good chance of getting it all."

"Wow!" said Samantha, shaking her head. "That would be a shame, Mom. Lots of needy people could be helped by that money."

"This Uriah guy doesn't sound very nice,

Mrs. Scarlet," said Wendy.

"No, Wendy, I'm afraid he isn't," Mrs. Scarlet continued. "He was never very nice to Mrs. Turquoise when she was alive. And now he's trying to get her money, her house, everything."

"Speaking of her house," said Peter, pointing out the car window, "there it is!"

The car pulled up to a huge mansion that was over one hundred years old. Ancient shutters hung from the windows, banging against the house in the wind.

"Wow!" shouted Polly. "Creepy-looking place."

"Wait until you see the *inside!*" said Samantha, who had been to the house a few times with her mother.

Everyone got out of the car and walked slowly to the large oak front door. A big, brass lion's head knocker stared down at them from the center of the door. Mrs. Scarlet put the key into the lock.

"You're right, Samantha," said Georgie, once they were all inside. "The inside *is* creepier."

Cobwebs hung from every corner. Strange shadows danced on the dust-covered furniture.

While Mrs. Scarlet fed the parrot, Gabe, the six friends wandered through the spooky house.

Georgie and Polly crept up a creaky old stairway. A series of portraits hung along the wall.

"Who are they?" asked Georgie, pointing to the paintings.

"They are probably members of the Turquoise family," explained Polly.

"A pretty dreary-looking bunch," said Georgie.

Peter and Samantha found a musty old trunk filled with photographs. "Judging from the clothing and furnishings, some of these pictures date back to the turn of the century," said Peter.

"Here's one of Mrs. Turquoise as a little girl," said Samantha. "I love looking at old photos."

Mortimer and Wendy walked over to Mrs. Turquoise's grand piano, sitting in the middle of the large room. Gabe squawked from his cage near the piano.

"Look at this," said Mortimer, pointing to a sheet of music paper propped up on the piano. "It's a handwritten piece of music. I didn't know Mrs. Turquoise wrote music."

"You can play the piano, Wendy," said Mrs. Scarlet. "Why don't you try playing what Mrs. Turquoise wrote?"

Wendy sat at the piano and began to play.

"That sounds terrible," teased Mortimer. "You're not playing it right."

"Try it again, Wendy," encouraged Mrs. Scarlet.

Wendy played the tune again. Again it sounded terrible.

"I don't know what's wrong," said Wendy. "I'm playing the notes that are written here." She pointed to the music sheet and followed the notes.

All of a sudden Gabe began whistling from his cage.

"Listen," said Wendy. "Gabe is whis-

tling the exact same tune. Note for note."
Wendy looked at the sheet music closely.
"Wait a minute," she cried. "Mrs. Scarlet,
I know where you can find the missing
will!"

**Where is the will, and how did Wendy
know where to find it?**

The Case of the Secret Message

"What do you mean, Wendy?" asked Mrs. Scarlet. "How can you possibly know where the will is?"

Wendy took the sheet music from the piano and brought it over to Mrs. Scarlet.

"Mrs. Turquoise wrote the location of the will into this page of music," explained Wendy. "Look at the notes. They are: G-A-B-E-C-A-G-E. No wonder the song sounded so terrible. It's not a song at all. She just used the musical notes to spell out 'Gabe Cage.' The will must be in Gabe's cage!"

Mrs. Scarlet took Gabe from his cage and placed him on a nearby perch. The parrot whistled the strange tune again. Mrs. Scarlet then looked under the plastic that lined the bottom of Gabe's cage and, sure enough, there was the missing will.

"Mrs. Turquoise *did* leave her money to

charity," said Mrs. Scarlet after reading the will. "Thanks, Wendy, you've just helped a lot of people who really need the help."